It all started w
~a nail-biting nove
2020

About the author
Aicha Balde is a 13year old girl that enjoys writing and learning new things so when she watched a documentary about locked in syndrome it inspired her to write a quick read for teens whilst shedding light on this syndrome.

She's alive!

Colors. I could only see colors. In a haze of panic and distress my eyes hastily searched the room for any idea of where I might be, the colors were starting to fade and soon became mere specks in the dark. I frantically tried to move or shout however nothing happened; nevertheless, I relentlessly kept trying my best to move at least one muscle in my body or call out to someone, I didn't stop until I felt one warm single tear roll down my cheek, I was so concentrated on finding a way to communicate with someone I didn't realize I was crying.

That's when reality hit me- wherever I am I'm trapped. On my own, leaving darkness as my only friend. I was about to accept my defeat until I saw some light seeping through the floor. A door-that I didn't realise was there- was being pushed open, in those few moments alone hundreds of questions appeared in my head, is that my mum? Do I know this person? Is it the person responsible for me being here? Will they tell me everything I need to know?

The list went on.

My ongoing curiosity was put to an end when the door revealed a nurse, why on earth was a nurse here? She was quickly followed by my mother and sister they had flicked the light switch on and I was able to study their faces my mother and sister looked like they hadn't slept in weeks, and the nurse, well she didn't look like a nurse, she just looked like a 20-year-old girl that decided to wear a nurse costume for Halloween. She had what seemed like a bucket load of makeup on so much that the makeup somehow managed to give the reverse effect of what makeup was supposed to do. Their distraught faces loomed over me, after what seemed like an age my sister broke the silence.

"her eyes moved, mum she's alive!"

 what did she mean by "she's alive" of course I'm alive, why am I in the hospital anyway, and?
Why can't I move my body? A worried look appeared on the nurse's face and she quickly
rushed out of the room.

 "Stupid woman, I bet she doesn't know what's even going on half the time"
 my Mum muttered she was never like this what on earth has gotten into her I barely
recognize her she looks so drained.
Before I could think of anything else the Nurse rushed in the room with a doctor following closely behind her.

 "Hello ladies, I'm Doctor Richards. I hear Hayley's eyes have started to have movement?"

While my mum and sister were murmuring yes, the nurse flicked on a flashlight in my eyes, I wanted to scream I can hear and see just get me out of here but no matter how hard I tried I couldn't even open my mouth. I used to have the best life; I closed my eyes.

*

I opened my eyes and I'm in my bedroom. I look over and my sisters still sound asleep on her bed, I check the time: 6:45 am. I put on my favorite fluffy jumper and go to brush my teeth and wash my face then mum calls us down for breakfast my sister brushes past me and goes downstairs I quickly follow behind her I can smell the sweet aroma of my mum's pancakes I go upstairs and start on my makeup and hair, my sister starts playing her music and singing off-key, I try my best to block out her awful voice and finish getting ready. I meet my best friend Liz and head off to school. I can still feel the warm sun from walking to school on the beautiful summer mornings.

*

"Hayley, Hayley?" Doctor Richards was so close I could feel his oddly ice-cold breath on my face, I did my best to squint, I was still adjusting to the agonizing light in my eyes "blink twice if you can hear me", why does he think I can't hear him?, my train of thoughts came to an abrupt pause when I realized there were many expectant faces peering at my eyes waiting for me to blink as if it was a scene in the finals of a tv show when they're about to announce the winner of the season, much to my annoyance I blinked followed by the heaviest sigh I could muster almost immediately a sigh of relief was let out by nearly everyone in that room. Doctor Richards sat my mum and sister down and started talking, unfortunately, I couldn't hear the whole conversation as I got an excruciating headache that caused a deafening ringing noise but I did manage to catch Doctor Richards saying

"she's making progress and will be back to normal in a year or less a year! I can't be stuck here for a year I- I- the room was spinning the walls was closing in it was becoming hard to breathe and then. Black. Pitch black.

Blink

I slowly opened my eyes, I had expected to see Dr Richards and that hideous nurse but Mum and Katie were just sat by my bedside neither of them had noticed me waking up and I obviously couldn't get their attention so I simply stared at the popcorn ceiling above me and tried to

comprehend the news
So, I'm stuck like this now. I guess' 'what
if I never get better?' 'what if I spend the
rest of my life paralysed?'

 Katie whispered "Mum I think she's
awake"

Mum lent over me and gave me a
comforting smile which was short-lived
"look Hun I don't know how to say this but
you have locked-in syndrome which is
basically you being trapped in your own
body." she said in between sobs "they
think it will take you about a year to get
your body to work again but you're going
to have to learn how to talk how to walk
and eat again." tears were streaming
down her face now.

I didn't know what to say. It's not like I could say anything. I think Mum caught on and said: "blink once if you're ok with this blink twice if you're unhappy blink three times if you're unsure." I blinked 5 times. I was unhappy and unsure which I think she expected although she probably would have hoped for only one blink.

"I understand darling," she whispered while stroking my head. "You're such a strong little girl, I don't know what I would've done if I were in your shoes."

I wanted to comfort Mum and tell her everything would be ok and that I'd be back to normal Hayley in no time but of course, I didn't instead I just lay there helpless wondering if I would ever be the same.

I think mum noticed I wasn't listening anymore and told me to get some rest and she was taking Katie to auntie Jems' house and would be right back. She asked me to blink once if I was okay with that and twice if I wasn't. I, of course, blinked once and Katie said goodbye and kissed my forehead whilst Mum kissed my cheek. I wanted to stay up until she came back but I could feel my eyes getting heavy and I fell into a deep sleep.

I had a nightmare- that I was stuck like this forever and my family lost hope and stopped visiting me and when they did, they would tell me how they were going to turn off the life support and hope I burn in hell for all the pain I caused. It was such a vivid dream that it was almost impossible to tell if it was real or not, but I somehow managed to wake up. My eyes shot open and I felt a lump in my throat and before I knew it tears were rolling down my cheek and I was too scared to go to sleep again so I just waited for mum to come back.

All in the head

I opened my eyes; I must've fallen asleep again. A part of me was sad that I wasn't able to stay awake till mum came back, I looked over to where she normally sits looking miserable but today was different, she looked ecstatic. Since I couldn't ask her why she was so happy I just stared at her to get her attention it took quite a while but she finally noticed me.

 "Hey, Hayley you're probably wondering why I'm so happy but when you passed out yesterday Dr Richards said it would be a perfect time to take a test to see how likely you'll be stuck like this and I spoke to him today and he said it's wonderful news but he wanted to tell us when we were together though." She said through smiling teeth.

 You would expect me to be happy for this but mum tends to make things seem a lot better than they are and get her hopes up just to be disappointed, for the first time I was glad I couldn't talk. 'Good news? He's probably going to say instead of me staying here for a year it's 9 months! As if that's any better.'

"Don't worry Hayley I know you're as anxious as I am to receive the news, but he's coming any minute now."

Good Lord the poor woman is more excited than I am!

"Hello ladies nice to see you again, I've come to give you your test results," said Dr Richards in his usual cheerful voice. "I was so shocked with these results I had to rerun the test again but alas they came back the same" he was smiling now " It turns out we misdiagnosed you, Hayley, yes, you may have the symptoms of the locked-in syndrome, but that's only because you think your trapped your results show that everything to do with this disease is all mental and if you trick your brain into thinking your body is working normally it will believe it and parts of your body will switch on again."

"How long will that take?" mum asked.

"It can take as short as one day or as long as one year it really depends how dedicated Hayley is to get back to her normal lieder Richards said looking at me. "Hayley blink once if you want to start this treatment now and blink twice if you want to do it tomorrow"

Are you kidding?! If there's a chance I can get out of here in less than a week I'm going to take it!

I, very happily, blinked once.
"Excellent news!" exclaimed Dr Richards "I'll bring nurse Kaiya in shortly to take you to the treatment rooms"

Empty book

A nurse walked in shortly after with the most gorgeous ebony skin and the type of smile that lit up a room. I was immensely relieved that I didn't get the nurse that looked like she was wearing a Halloween costume.

"Hi Hayley, I'm Martha, Blink once if you're ready to go to your treatment," she said smiling.

"Martha we've already asked and she said that she's ready," Dr Richards said in a 'matter of fact' tone.

"My bad" Martha was scowling now; I don't know why but I feel like something went down between them. I'll have to ask Martha when I can talk again. "I'm going to wheel you out on your bed sweetheart as we are not strong enough to move you onto a wheelchair but when you get some movement back in your legs again, you'll be wheeling around in no time," She said chuckling.

It was Dr Richards turn to scowl now "If you enable her to abuse the privileges that come with the wheelchair then we might as well get a new nurse"

"That won't be necessary Will," Martha said, shooting him a death stare."

She called him by his first name, do they know each other personally?

Before Dr Richards could say anything else me and Martha had left. This was my first time outside of my hospital room, it was a shame I couldn't look around properly, there was a strong scent of hand-sanitizer and disinfectant wipes.

Martha wheeled me into the prettiest room, it was bright airy and had so many cute little decorations and said 'Hayley's room' on the front I shared a room back home so this was amazing. Martha placed a notebook in my lap and said: "I know I don't know you personally dear, but you seem like a survivor and you have what it takes to be back to normal by tomorrow, I know Will told you it would take a little bit longer but were going to prove them, wrong Hun, ok?"

She used very odd tactics, to help me to talk again she told me to tell myself I can talk and to imagine saying the word cat and how my mouth would move, to get me to walk again she made me close my eyes and imagine I was running in a marathon and to get me to move my arms and hands again she told me to imagine catching and throwing a ball. None of which worked because I was still paralyzed.

"Hayley, I can see the frustration in your eyes darling, these treatments barely work right away for people but by tomorrow I'm expecting you to have written an account of everything that's happened to you from when you arrived here up to this point," she said.

This woman must be crazy, does she not realise I'm PARALYSED?

"It sounds crazy I know but trust me the lord is looking over you I can feel it," she said now wheeling me out.

So, I tried to make a little prayer to god in my head but ended up falling asleep instead you'd think being paralysed stores all your energy but it just drained mine.

Miracle

I woke up and something was...different.
I had a similar perplexing feeling to that
which I felt on the night I woke up here
and I didn't like it. Something told me to
at least try and move a muscle to see if
the treatment worked. It was almost too
easy. My voice was the same. I had no
difficulty moving or speaking so I
naturally thought I was dreaming so I
pinched myself, yep definitely real-life
now.
Instead of just sitting and waiting I
decided to write that account of my time
here from the beginning to the end and
that's what you're reading now. Dr
Richards claimed it to be a miracle whilst
Martha said it was inevitable.

I stood up to go wake my mum up. I was so overwhelmed I didn't realise I was crying.

"Hayley what's wrong, what you can walk you're okay you're okay!" Mum exclaimed "Let me get Dr Richards and the nurse"

Instead of just sitting and waiting I decided to write that account of my time here from the beginning to the end and that's what you're reading now. Dr Richards claimed it to be a miracle whilst Martha said it was inevitable.

We left the hospital and everything went back to normal like it never changed. I hope Martha likes this account of my time there. And I hope the next time I go to a hospital is when I give birth ha-ha.

Printed in Great Britain
by Amazon